The Carriage Twins Very First Adventure

The Carriage Twins Very First Adventure

Co Authored by
Janet L. Pallo and Judith A. Kaminski
Twin Owners of the
Victorian Carriage Museum

Illustrator
Michael R. Miller

Dedicated to Twins Everywhere

Special Dedication To
Logan D. Pallo
and
Xavier M. Pallo

Library of Congress Control Number: 2009935447
ISBN: 978-0-9842277-0-9

Printed by:
BookMasters, Inc.
30 Amberwood Parkway
Ashland, OH 44805
December 2009
M6811

About the Authors

Judith Kaminski and Janet Pallo are identical twins born and raised in the Great Lakes region of Ashtabula, Ohio. Even as young grade schoolers they had dreamed of becoming teachers and business owners.

Their love of children and a passionate desire to collect Victorian art saw them fulfilling their far reaching goals.

Judy and Jan earned their undergraduate degrees at Kent State University in Ohio and then went on to receiving their masters degrees in education from Lake Erie College. In 1988 they opened The Victorian Perambulator Museum in Jefferson, Ohio.

Their teaching careers spanned more than thirty years and their unique Victorian Art collection has resulted in a one-of-a-kind museum that focuses on the child's life in the Victorian Era.

The museum houses over 200 carriages as well as antique dolls of the period. A myriad of toys, antique toys, sleighs, vintage clothes, and books showcase their extensive presentation.

Teaching their pupils to become high achievers and avid readers led the sisters to turn to writing. Having co-authored two books about Victorian carriages, they decided to utilize their talents by writing a children's fantasy which would include their carriages, antique dolls, and carrousel horses to create a delightful story.

The idea of a magical adventure with identical twins Penelope and Priscilla as their main characters lends itself to unlimited future carriage adventures.

About the Illustrator

Born (1949) and raised in Sarasota, Florida, during the '50s and '60s, Mike was well aware of the creative environment around him. Artists, writers and free spirits surrounded him throughout his childhood and youth. Mike's interest in the graphic arts developed early, and Sarasota held a wealth of inspiration to draw from.

After receiving his B.F.A. from the University of South Florida, he continued to work on his painting skills even as life beckoned him north to Maine and New Hampshire. The American impressionist and the Ashcan school replaced his early heroes Van Gogh, Monet and Pissarro. Soon lesser-known New England painters like Gruppe, Hibbard and Thieme caught his attention and their wintertime connections to Florida stirred a longing to return to the Gulf Coast.

Mike returned to the Sarasota area in the mid-'80s and immediately began plein-aire, painting hometown scenes and memories of his youth. In 2002 Mike devoted himself full time to learning a more commercial approach to his art and his talent expanded. As his creative energy focused, his local success opened a platform for Mike's work to be viewed nationally as well as internationally. Dramatic light and composition skills keep the paintings fresh and engaging, ensuring years of enjoyment for their owners.

Always inspired, he will continue to paint colorful Florida landscapes, vivid florals and the small-town charm of local scenes. This is not only for the enjoyment of the present but the preservation for the future as well.

Dreams do come true when you believe in

Magic!

Once upon a time there were two extraordinary twins named Penelope and Priscilla. Now, they were not just adorable twins, in fact they were as special as two little girls could be.

The twins shared a secret beyond all secrets, and possibly, just maybe they were ready to share their secret for the very first time.

It just so happens that Penelope and Priscilla had a secret castle deep in the woods behind the elegant Victorian mansion that they now live in.

The Victorian mansion they live in with their wealthy parents is as fancy as anyone could imagine. In fact it is so fancy admirers would exclaim, "I wonder who would ever live in such a fabulous mansion?"

Now, the twins never bragged about their elegant home. They wanted others to think they were ordinary young girls. They tried to fit in with other children their age, however this was just not to be.

There were boys and girls that would whisper behind their backs. They told tales about how Penelope and Priscilla were very unusual and strange. Consequently, no other children would play with them.

Penelope and Priscilla had been treated differently all of their lives, but they didn't seem to mind, well, they sometimes minded.

Being the special young ladies that they were, they overcame their feelings of neglect by traveling to their secret castle deep in the woods.

Today, was to be different from all other days, because they were to share their first real adventure from the castle.

Automatically, as they whispered the secret code the doors flew open. Much to the amazement of Penelope and Priscilla they threw up their hands in delight to see the wonderful carriages awaiting them. The carriages were awaiting with excited anticipation, hoping to be chosen for the twins first adventure.

Each carriage was a sight to behold. There were carriages that looked like swans, and those that resembled peacocks, butterflies, gondolas, antique cars, and on, and on, and on. They were so special, the twins had to ponder and ponder before they both decided at the very same time, as twins often do that one of them was more special than the others.

The day was the 29th of February and it was going to be one of the most exciting days of their lives.

The twins announced to their awesome, one-of-a-kind museum of carriages, that their choice for their first big adventure would have to be "The Sultan", the treasure of all carriages. They assured the others that they would indeed have their own adventure in the future.

The Sultan came rolling out bursting to the seams with pride at having been chosen for their very first adventure.

Now, Penelope and Priscilla both were thinking out loud. We must surprise our beloved set of twin dolls at once, that they will be invited to travel with us on the adventure of a lifetime. The dolls will certainly want to look their very best! They so love to please us!

We must be careful not to tell them too much, or they will brag to the other dolls about their good fortune.

So, Penelope and Priscilla prepared to embark on their first adventure that would transport them to another land far, far away.

MILLER

With the lovely twin dolls now cozily beside them in the magnificent Sultan, they were as ready as they could be. How grand they appeared as the Sultan lifted off from the castle terrace ever so lightly. The sky sparkled with the full moon, and the radiant stars were twinkling as far as the eyes could see.

Within a very short time the Sultan seemed to be slowing ever so gently, while four pairs of eyes were wide open with astonishment at what they were experiencing.

All of a sudden the Sultan leaped upward, and then plummeted toward the most beautiful fantasyland anyone could possibly imagine! It was like being in a world filled with spectacular mystical rides that seemed to go on as far as the eyes could see!

Magnificent, was the word that popped out of Penelope and Priscilla's mouths at the exact same time. Not only were their mouths wide open, their eyes just sparkled with excitement and awe in anticipation for what was in store for them.

The twins held on to their dolls as tight as they could manage, for they feared that they would leap right out of their arms in their eagerness to experience the fun awaiting them.

The Sultan came to an abrupt halt right in the middle of the spectacular wonderland. Along with their dolls the girls promptly scurried out of their carriage and glanced every which way. Deciding at the exact same time, they dashed towards the huge roller coaster that was anxiously awaiting their arrival.

Penelope and Priscilla, along with their beloved dolls jumped into the first seat and held on for dear life. Up, up they went and before they could catch their breath down they flew, and immediately up again, then round, and round, and down once more, until yet another hill. They squealed with sure delight with each and every thrill. Finally, the roller coaster came to a screeching halt right in front of the most amazing magical carrousel that they had ever seen!

The giant carrousel exceeded any description one could imagine. Dashing as quickly as their legs could carry them, they scurried faster and faster toward their favorite horse when "Ka Pow!" The girls collided with one another including the dolls. Laughing so hard they were rolling on their sides with the dolls cradled in their arms. They indeed, desired the huge black and gold Victorian mare over all the rest. She was the most outstanding horse on the carrousel. She had a magical twinkle in her eye!

Once they had managed to climb on and grasp her reins she leaped, and soared high above the other horses while they stared in awe! The horses chanted, "Victoria, take care of the girls and dolls!"

Victoria whinnied her assurance.

The ride lasted just long enough to satisfy their desires. The entire park below sparkled like jewels, shimmering in colorful lights. Victoria brought them back ever so gently, they barely felt the landing on the musical carrousel.

Whimsically, they floated off Victoria into a fluffy cloud that reminded them of their favorite cotton candy.

Before they knew what was happening they were back in the Sultan soaring away from their fantastic adventure.

Penelope and Priscilla were truly saddened at the thought of leaving the magical park, but they knew deep in their hearts that all special adventures come to an end. The girls knew however, that there would be more to follow.

As the Sultan guided them back to the castle the young ladies chatted on and on about their first adventure. The twins vowed to keep their secret adventure to themselves, and the dolls agreed.

As the Sultan landed gentle as a feather touching the ground, Penelope and Priscilla glanced up in the sky one last time. Before entering the castle the moon winked at them, and they both together winked back with smiling glimmering faces.

They stepped off the Sultan and immediately started cleaning and shining it until the Sultan sparkled. The dolls clapped with delight at their efforts!

The first adventure exceeded their expectations. They wondered how they would ever top it!

Bidding their dolls and the Sultan an affectionate farewell the twins quietly slipped out of their fairytale castle and tiptoed back to the family mansion. They climbed up the secret stairway without waking their sleeping parents.

The twins parents never worried about them, because they trusted them to always do the right thing, no matter what!

Finally, all snuggled under their look alike down feathered quilts they reached out their dainty hands, and gave each other their special squeeze and their magical star sparkled with love.

"Until our next

Magical

Adventure!

We can hardly wait!"

"Can you?"

"Hold on to your star until then!"